MW01013295

Puppa-na-wuppana

The Beagle with the Magical Nose

by Cindy Koebele & Lori Weaver

Illustrated by Michael Laduca

Koebele Weaver Enterprises, LLC
720 Arcwood Road
Mahtomedi, MN 55115
www.koebeleweaver.com

Book design and illustrations by Michael LaDuca, Luminus Media LLC

ISBN: 978-0-9909202-0-5

Library of Congress Control Number: 2014919174

Printed in the United States of America

My name is **Puppa-na-wuppana.**

Sometimes I am called **PuppyWuppie** or just **Puppa.**

I hear that I am a Beagle dog. I do not know what that means.

I do know that I am very special and I lead a very special life.
You could say I am "charmed".

I have a special nose that can smell everything!
I think it is **magical.**

I find lots of things to play with and chew on and eat with my **magical nose**.

This sometimes gets me into **trouble**.

I have a **Mom** and two **brothers**, Alec and Andre.

I was just a baby when they came and **adopted** me from my Beagle Mom.

I was **scared** at first, but after lots of **kisses** and **snuggling**, I knew this was where I belonged.

When I was a **baby**, my teeth hurt while they were growing in.

Chewing on things made them feel so much better.

Each day I looked around for **something new to chew on** but sometimes I was **scolded** for what I chewed on.

This made me **sad.**

Why can't I chew on Mom's shoes...or the furniture...or **all the great things** Alec and Andre leave on the floor? Aren't these gifts for me?

And what is this "puppy" stage I keep hearing about? I don't know, I am just me...

Puppa-na-Wuppana and I am special.

Oh, and **Keekers!** She is one of my very best friends!

She was already **part of my family** the day I arrived.

She is **black and furry** and she makes a strange noise when she is happy.

It sounds like **Prrrrrrrrrrrrrrrrr.**

It was love at first sight for **Keekers and me!**
We looked into each other's eyes, she batted my arm with
her paw and off **we ran to play.**

Sometimes we play so hard, that Mom says we are silly and to stop fighting like **"cats and dogs"**.

We do not listen. We are **having too much fun**.

Our favorite game is **Hide and Seek**.
Keekers is **very, very good** at this game.
She knows all the best spots to hide and
she can climb!

I cannot climb...but, she is no match for my **magical Beagle nose!!**

Sniff, Sniff ...I can always find her!

At first, Mom tried to have me sleep in a **box** she called a **kennel**.

I did not like this **kennel box**.

It was lonely. I **cried and cried** for my family and I did not sleep all night long.

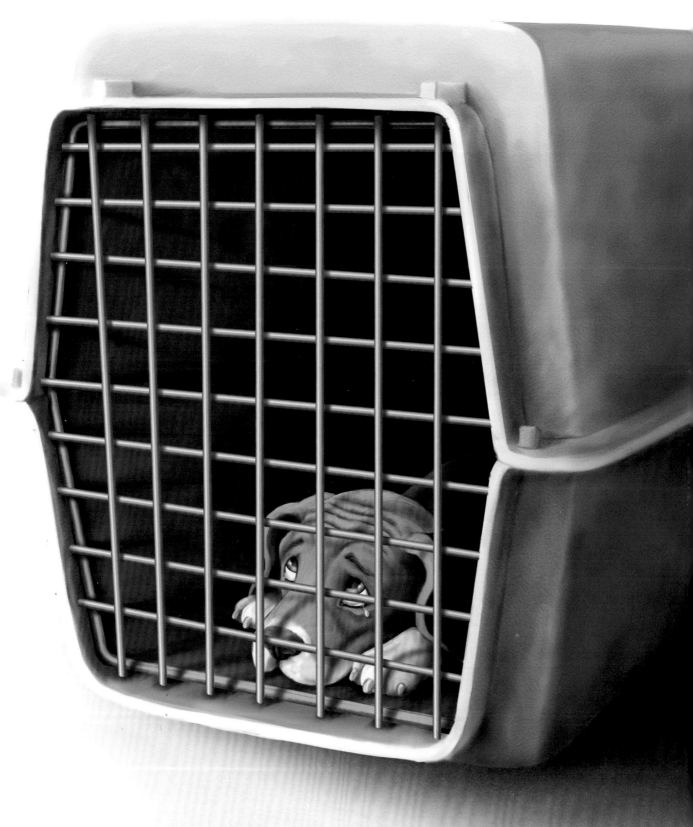

I guess my family did not sleep all night long either, because now I sleep in a **big soft bed with my brothers**.

Sometimes, **Keekers** shares her spot at the end of Mom's bed with me if I ask her to.

Where else would a **special Beagle** with a

When the weather is nice, I go on lots of **walks around my neighborhood.**

Everyone we meet says, **"He is so cute!"** and asks "What is his name?"

When Mom says, **"It is Puppa-na-wuppana",** the children always giggle, tilt their head and say, "Puppa-na-na-na-na-wupp-ana? That is so special!"

I hold my head up high and wag my tail. Of course it is **special**

My name is **Puppa-na-wuppana**
and **I** am special!